I0540145

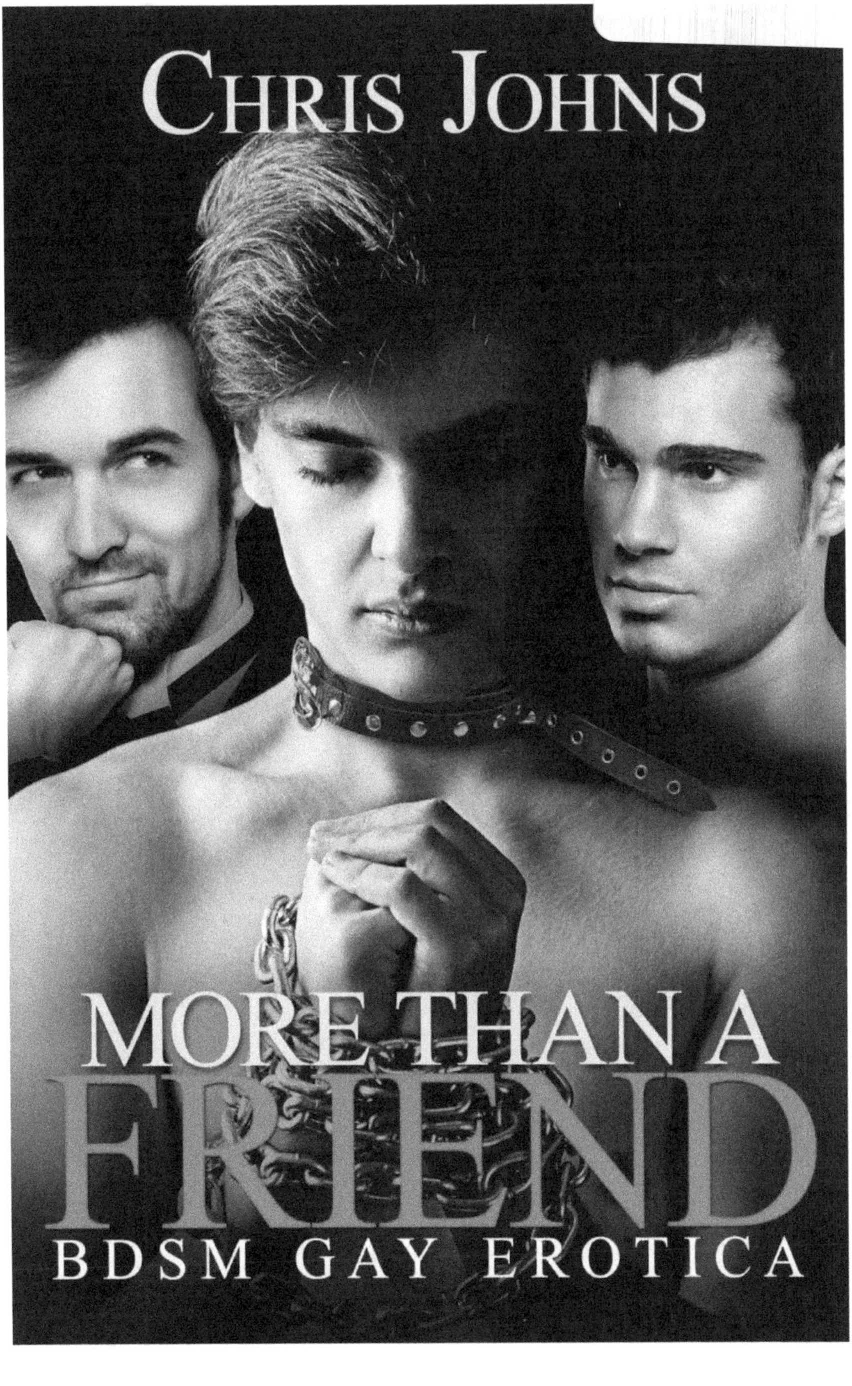

CHRIS JOHNS

MORE THAN A FRIEND

BDSM GAY EROTICA

WARNING

This book contains sexually explicit scenes and adult language. It may be considered offensive to some readers. This book is for sale to adults ONLY.

* * * * * * * * * * * * * * * * * * *

Please store your files wisely where they cannot be accessed by underage readers.

Please feel free to send me an email. Just know that these emails are filtered by my publisher. Good news is always welcome.

Chris Johns - **chris_johns@awesomeauthors.org**

You might also want to check my blog for Updates and interesting info.
http://chris-johns.awesomeauthors.org/

Copyright © 2014 by Chris Johns

All Rights reserved under International and Pan-American Copyright Conventions. By payment of required fees you have been granted the non-exclusive, non-transferable right to access and read the text of this book. No part of this text may be reproduced, transmitted, downloaded, decompiled, reverse-engineered or stored in or introduced into any information storage and retrieval system, in any form or by any means, whether electronic or mechanical, now known, hereinafter invented, without express written permission of 4Fun Publishing. For more information contact 4Fun Publishing. The publisher does not have any control over and does not assume any responsibility for author or third-party websites or their content. This book is a work of fiction. The characters, incidents and dialogue are drawn from the author's imagination and are not to be construed as real. While reference might be made to actual historical events or existing locations, the names, characters, places and incidents are either products of the author's imagination or are used fictitiously, and any resemblance to actual persons living or dead, business establishments, events or locales is entirely coincidental.

About the Publisher

4Fun Publishing, a member of **BLVNP Incorporated**, 340 S. Lemon #6200, Walnut CA 91789, info@blvnp.com / legal@blvnp.com
NOTE: Due to the highly emotional reaction of some people to works of erotic fiction, any email sent to the above address that contains foul language or religious references is automatically deleted by our anti-spam software and will not be seen. All other communications are welcome.

DISCLAIMER

Please don't be stupid and kill yourself. This book is a work of FICTION. Do not try any new sexual practice that you find in this book. It is fiction and not to be confused with reality. Neither the author nor the publisher or its associates assume any responsibility for any loss, injury, death or legal consequences resulting from acting on the contents in this book. Every character in this book is over 18 years of age. The author's opinions are not to be construed as the opinions of the publisher. The material in this book is for entertainment purposes ONLY. Enjoy.

More Than A Friend

BDSM Gay Erotica

By: Chris Johns

© Chris Johns 2014
ISBN: 978-1-62761-944-8

Part 1
Matt's Abduction

Jack Rushton had made his millions on the back of hard working and loyal staff. He never forgot that, and those who remained, and had gone through the lean years with him, were now regularly rewarded with fat bonuses. He didn't just throw money at these people, though; he also looked out for their welfare.

Mark Stator was one of those people, and Jack knew all was not well in the Stator household. Mark's wife had died a couple of years ago, leaving him with a teenage son to bring up.

Jack wanted to help and sent for Mark to see what the problem was.

"Come in, Mark; sit down. Coffee?"

"Yes please, Jack."

The two men sat opposite each other in easy chairs in Jack's office.

"I don't want to interfere in your personal life, Mark, but I've noticed you are looking a bit care worn these days. Is there anything I can do to help?"

Mark slumped down in his chair and with a big sigh unloaded his problem.

"Not really, Jack. My boy is going off the rails a bit, and I can't seem to communicate with him anymore."

"Hmm, not an unusual situation. Like to tell me a little more?"

"Well, he's joined some punk rock band, and gone a bit overboard to fit in. Lots of tattoos and body piercings, but worst of all he's had his earlobes extended and looks like a Masai. Employers are put off, so he can't get a proper job, and the band doesn't make much either. I know he's smoking way too much pot, and I'm worried he'll move on to harder drugs. I just don't know how to get through to him that he's ruining his life."

Jack thought about it while the two of them finished their coffees.

"Let me think about this Mark; perhaps I can come up with something."

He had already come up with something, but Mark wouldn't know about it until it happened.

"SKY, I want you to pick up a young man called Matt Stator. Take him out to the villa and sort him out."

Jack wasn't wasting any time; he had talked to his fixer within a few minutes of Mark leaving his office. Sky didn't waste any time either.

That night, after Matt and his band finished their gig, Matt slid out of the back door of the club to smoke a joint. He was cursing the new government regulation that forbade smoking in a public place. As he smoked, an SUV with darkened windows pulled up and two men opened a door. Before Matt knew what was happening, he was bundled into the vehicle and driven off.

Twenty four hours later, when a missing person report was filed, and the story from a band member had been analyzed, a half smoked joint was found at the rear entrance to the club, and DNA confirmed that Matt had been smoking it.

Jack again sent for Mark.

"I'm not going to tell you anything, Mark, except that I don't want you to worry about Matt. He is safe and well. When you get him back, I promise you will be pleased." Mark looked deep into the eyes of his boss and just nodded his head.

"Thank you, Jack. You will see he is treated right, won't you?"

"Of course, Mark; you have my word."

That was good enough for Mark, and he stopped worrying, got on with his job, and left his son's fate in Jack's hands.

MATT WOKE up feeling like a million dollars. The usual fuzzy head from smoking too much pot after a gig was gone. Half a joint was not going to affect him, and that was all he had time for before he was abducted. He got up, walked over to the window, and looked down on a beautiful garden with a large kidney shaped swimming pool in the center.

He quickly realized that he could not possibly still be in England; the temperature was as high as a hot summer day, but it was only March. Also, the vegetation was hardly England…palms and cacti weren't a regular feature at home. He didn't have to wonder for long. As he turned to explore his surroundings, the door opened and a giant of a man came in, fully clothed, and Matt, realized he was naked and tried to cover himself as the man mountain approached him.

"My name is Alexander. My master wishes you to join him by the pool, but you must first shower, shave and clean your teeth. I will be back for you in fifteen minutes; be ready."

With that, Alexander turned and walked out. Matt was dumb struck, but tried to follow. The door was locked, and the other door led to the bathroom where everything he needed was laid out.

Might as well do as I'm asked; I need a shower anyway, was the thought that ran through Matt's head as he sniffed his armpits.

Fifteen minutes later Alexander was back.

"Come with me," was all he said.

"But I have no clothes."

"You won't need them."

"But—"

"No buts, boy; do as you are told and come with me."

Feeling extremely embarrassed, Matt did as he was told. He had to find out what was going on, and the only way he could think to do that was to talk to the man by the pool.

Matt was nineteen and guessed the man on the sun bed to be about ten years older. As he approached, keeping a little behind Alexander, Matt noted the man, as he stood up, was probably an inch or two taller than him, well put together, without being over muscled. He couldn't see the eyes, which were covered with a pair of designer sun glasses, but noted the mid brown hair and the aquiline features, the golden tan with a dusting of hair on the chest, and, finally, the very pronounced bulge in his Speedos. He wasn't quite sure why his brain noted that fact particularly; men had never held his interest; women hadn't either, but he thought that being spaced out on drugs so often had put his sexual desires to sleep.

He stopped in front of the man and started to speak, but the man put a finger to his lips and stood in front of him.

"Listen, Matt, and learn. You will speak when spoken to, and you will obey every order given to you by me or my staff."

Matt interrupted, "Who the fuck are you?"

It was definitely the wrong thing to say. The man nodded, and before Matt could react, Alexander had him bent over a poolside table and delivered ten very hard slaps with his hand to Matt's bare arse.

Alexander was probably about six feet six inches tall, and around 225 pounds of what looked like solid muscle. A spanking from those hands was not something to want twice. Matt was howling when he was again stood facing the man, tears streaming down his face.

"As I was saying, you will call me Master at all times, and Alexander you will address as Sir. If you wish to speak, other than to answer a question, you will ask, 'Permission to speak, Master, or Sir', and wait to be given permission before continuing. If you utter any more profanities, you will be punished. Do you understand those instructions?"

Matt felt resentful, and made his second mistake.

"Yes," he mumbled.

Alexander was on him in a flash, delivering another very hard swat to his already very red ass. Matt yelped and jumped forward, almost knocking the Master over.

"Yes, what, Matt?" The man barked out.

"Yes, Master," was the now much more precise reply.

"Good. Now then, we are going to start cleaning you up before trying to turn you back into a civilised human being, inside as well. When I am finished, you will go with Alex. All of those disgusting bits of metal on you will be removed, and you will be given a respectable haircut. Then you can rejoin me for lunch. Tomorrow, you will be taken to a hospital for plastic surgery to restore your ear lobes to their proper shape. The following day, you will undergo laser treatment to remove all those tattoos, and then we will be left with a human being on the outside, instead of some painted and pierced animal. We will then spend however long we have to, training you to return to society as a useful and civilized person. Do you understand?"

Matt was fuming! "You can't do that! Let me go! You have no right to do this!" He was almost beside himself with anger, but not for long. Alexander was on him again and delivered another ten very hard slaps to a pair of cheeks already showing bruising from the first ten. Stood in front of the Master again, Matt was informed that there would be no more bare hand spankings.

"If you need chastising again, Matt, it will be with a cane. Do you understand?"

Through his sobs, Matt replied with a shaking voice, "Yes, Master."

"Good boy; now off you go with Alex."

As Matt followed Alex from the pool, Sky, the master, watched the retreating figures, and thought what a cute butt Matt had, and how much cuter it would look if he gave it a chance to return to its normal color.

When Matt returned to join Sky for lunch, the improvement was already quite dramatic. A neat college boy haircut, all the body piercings removed, the result was amazing! The ears were quite awful, but tomorrow they would be improved as well.

"Come here, Boy; stand there," Sky said, pointing to a spot in front of him. "Put your hands behind your head and stand with your feet apart. Do not move until I tell you to." Matt looked worried, particularly when Alexander stood beside him holding a long cane.

"Remember, boy, don't move." Alex swished the cane through the air to emphasize his remark.

Sky started at the neck and ran his hands all over Matt's body, front and rear. When he lifted the boy's cock, to have a look at the place where the Prince Albert had been, Matt nearly died with the embarrassment. He blushed a deep scarlet and broke out into a sweat, but he didn't move. He was wound up as tight as a watch spring, though. The inspection continued, with his balls being lifted and inspected, before being told to bend over and spread his legs further to make his anus visible. He was so tempted to challenge this order, but, again, the swish of the cane stopped him from doing so. Sky ran his hand over the bruised cheeks, and then slid a finger into the crack and put pressure on Matt's anal entry.

"Are you a virgin here, Matt?"

Matt gulped and then replied, "Yes, Master."

"Alright, stand up again, hands behind your head."

Walking round in front of Matt again, Sky noted that the boy would not look him in the eyes. He knew there was a good mixture of shame and embarrassment involved, which was precisely what he had intended.

"Well done, Boy. You don't like pain do you?"

Matt shook his head, and then quickly remembered and said, "No, Master."

"That is good, because I don't like inflicting it. Now, shorts and T-shirt on the chair there; put them on and join me for lunch."

Matt's eyes followed the direction of Sky's finger and went over to dress. He immediately felt a million per cent better with clothes on. Rejoining Sky, he was directed to the chair opposite, where an air cushion had been placed, and, on cue, a waiter came in carrying plates of salad and cold meats. Matt realized then that he was hungry. A pleasant meal, washed down with fresh fruit juice and water, left Matt feeling very contented physically, but still very worried about where this was all headed. He was also, very resentful that his appearance was being changed dramatically without his consent. When coffee was served, and Sky started talking.

"I work out most days in the gym, Matt, and swim every day. You are going to do the same. You are also going to sunbathe a little every day as well. We are going to get rid of that pasty white color, all except a small patch that your Speedos will cover. Alex."

Alexander produced a neat pair of Speedos that looked far too small, but Sky told him to get undressed again, and put them on. Matt blushed again, disrobing while the other two watched. The fit was perfect; the pouch looked tailor made for his package, and felt very comfortable.

"Hmm, I think this young man will look very sexy, Alex, when we have put a little muscle, and a little color, on him."

"I agree, Sir; he is a very attractive young man."

Matt was surprised to be praised in this manner, having never thought very much about his appearance before, clothed or unclothed.

"Give lunch a chance to settle, Matt, and we will see how good you are in the water."

Matt smiled. Swimming was his only sporting accomplishment. He could swim forever, and was quite fast over short distances. An hour of sunbathing while lunch settled and Sky suggested a swim.

"Longest part of the pool, Matt; Alexander will count. We are going to do fifty lengths. Think you can make that?"

Matt looked at the pool and grinned, "Oh yes, Master; no problem."

No problem was correct. Matt had been sat on the edge of the pool for several minutes before Sky finished.

"Well done, boy; you certainly showed me the way home."

Matt was so pleased to be praised, even in this offhand manner, and couldn't resist making a comment about age slowing some people down. Wrong thing to say; Sky disliked comments that put him down.

"Let me show you about age, boy, and respect. Come with me."

The tone of voice made Matt realize his comment was ill formed.

"I'm sorry, Master; I didn't intend to be rude."

"I don't believe you, boy; you need to learn respect."

WITH ALEXANDER bringing up the rear, the three of them retired to a room in the house Matt had not previously seen. He didn't like the view at all. Sky threw him a towel.

"Speedos off and dry yourself."

The two men were stood, arms folded, watching the boy, once again naked, drying himself. As soon as he was finished, Alexander moved in and fitted a collar round his neck and two padded cuffs to his wrists. A short chain on each cuff was clipped onto rings on the collar so that, effectively, Matt was defenseless. He was walked across the room to a bench at about waist height and bent over it. A strap was secured over him at chest level, his legs were spread, and each ankle was locked into restraints set at the end of a four-foot bar attached to the base of the bench. Now completely immobilised, Matt was very frightened.

"Thank you, Alexander. You can leave us now. I will call you when you are needed to take this object back to his room."

As soon as the door closed, Sky addressed Matt.

"What I am going to do now I hope will be seared into your brain, boy, because I want to get your body fit very quickly, and that will not be possible if you are bruised and sore all the time. When Alexander returns, you will be of no use to me for maybe as long as a week. If I have to punish you again, that time span will double. You have to learn respect for your elders, and your betters, Matt, or you are going to be severely damaged goods."

Matt was shaking now and looking round to see what was coming. He saw Sky pick up the cane that Alexander had carried.

"Ten, Matt."

With no more ado, Sky positioned himself and administered the first stroke. Matt heard it coming and tensed his bottom muscles. When it struck, the pain was unbelievable. He was unable to scream for several seconds; nothing in his world had prepared him for this level of pain. Sky waited a full minute before delivering the next one. This time the scream was almost instantaneous, followed by a very broken plea.

"Oh God, Master, please; no more. I promise I will be good."

The pain was spreading throughout his body like a forest fire, and Matt thought he would die long before he had received all ten. The third one landed, and he passed out. As soon as he was conscious again, Sky delivered the fourth one. He was good; each stroke was equally spaced from the top of Matt's bottom, with the fourth one about four inches down. Again, Matt lost consciousness as he screamed. Awake again, and he took the fifth one, Sky lay it perfectly across the other four to produce the classic five barred gate. Matt was now swimming in a sea of pain he could barely believe. On recovery from that one, he couldn't speak, he was sobbing so hard. He was also shaking so hard he was almost breaking his restraints. No more came. Instead, he felt something cold on his buttocks and Sky's hands rubbing them.

He screamed at first, because even a gentle touch was agony, but not for long. The cream had a cooling effect on his bottom, and the anaesthetic in it quickly took away the worst of the pain. He relaxed onto the bench and allowed Sky to continue pampering him.

Sky had become extremely hard looking at the boy's bottom; it was seriously cute. Matt had a slim waist and narrow hips, making his bottom very slim, but nicely rounded, no doubt because of his swimming. When he had finished applying the healing and soothing salve, he slid a finger all the way down the crack from top to bottom, lightly touching the anal entry on the way and finishing by stroking the boy's balls.

"**I AM** going to make a decision on the final five later, Matt. Whether you get them or not will depend on you."

Matt breathed a sigh of relief. The pain was now just a dull ache; the fingers now playing with him were very comforting, even though they were touching places no one had ever touched before.

Sky continued stroking the boy, worrying his anus, and stroking all the way through between his legs to play with a flaccid penis that, nonetheless, felt extremely erotic.

Matt knew that what was being done to him was wrong, but it felt so nice, he wondered why he had never had anyone to do that to him before. Ten minutes of the stroking eventually had its effect, and the once flaccid penis showed signs of life. Sky loved it; as it grew, he used both hands and caressed more of Matt, surprised at the silkiness of the boy's skin. He may have been abusing his body with drugs, but he had not been doing it for long enough to ruin the skin texture.

Sky stood back, removed his Speedos, retrieved a bottle of lube from a shelf nearby, and moved back to Matt.

Matt felt the cold touch to his anus, followed almost instantly by Sky's finger rubbing gently round the lip and being inserted inside. He gasped and tensed.

"Relax, boy, you are going to enjoy this, but not if you tense up."

"But that is wrong, Master. Please don't put your finger in me."

"Shh, relax, enjoy."

Sky buried his finger a little deeper, moving it around, but being gentle. He soon had the whole finger inside Matt, and started to finger fuck him with it, eventually adding a second finger, and then a third. With three going in and out and being spread and twisted, Matt was amazed how good it felt, particularly coupled with Sky's other hand still playing fast and loose with his cock and balls.

Sky moved back a little to get a better look at Matt' bottom, and marveled at its perfection. He prayed that he would not have to punish it again, but for today he was going to take Matt's virginity. He lubed his penis, and put some more lube inside Matt. Moving close again, he placed his cock head against the anal entry of his captive, stroking his back, and telling him to relax. Applying pressure, he forced his head over the boy's sphincter, and held still. Matt screamed and begged Sky to take it out.

"Relax, boy; the pain will ease." As he spoke, he stroked and caressed the boy's body, and kept talking to him gently, until he felt his muscles relax. Then he fed him some more cock, a little at a time, until he was fully inserted.

"Relax, boy, you have all of me now. I'm going to slide in and out of you."

Matt was aware that what was happening to him was wrong. This man should not be fucking him, but at the same time what he was feeling defied belief. It felt so incredibly sensual; he was as hard as he had ever been, and Sky was still playing with him, making it even better.

When he felt Sky's cock sliding in and out, he opened his eyes wide and thought he would die of pleasure. His G spot was being assaulted on every stroke, and he started to orgasm. His screams now were of pleasure rather than pain.

"Oh, Master, fuck me harder; fuck me!"

The orgasms continued, forcing him to clench and unclench his glutes, taking Sky over the top as well. He pumped jet after jet of spunk into the boy in one of the fiercest orgasms he could ever remember.

Sky fell across Matt's body and nibbled on his ear before whispering to him.

"You are an amazing young man; that was incredible. Relax, I'm going to release you now."

Sky undid all the restraints, and gently lifted Matt into his arms.

"Come, we'll shower."

He walked Matt through to the shower, and stood him under the warm jets, letting the heat soak into his bones before washing him thoroughly. Matt was like putty in his hands, completely compliant. When they were both dry, Sky took the boy by the hand and led him back to his room.

"Sleep now, boy; we will talk again later."

Matt was asleep before Sky had left the room, a sleep of contentment, despite the stiffness of his lower parts from the beating.

It was dark when Matt woke and he was disoriented. As his thoughts came together, he remembered the afternoon. The satisfaction at beating Sky in the swimming, the incredible pain of the cane, and, lastly, the incredible sensations involved with being raped. Was he gay?

He had enjoyed the feel of Sky's penis inside him so much he had multiple orgasms. This was all so new. He rolled over and realized Sky was sat on the side of his bed.

"Hello, Boy; how do you feel?"

At the same time, he ran his hand through Matt's hair, and gently down the side of his face to his neck and shoulder.

"I'm a little stiff, Master, and my bottom hurts outside and in." Matt kept his eyes lowered; he couldn't look at this man again, not yet.

"Roll onto your tummy; I will put some more cream on it."

Sky pulled the sheet off Matt as he rolled over, turned on the bedside light, and started to caress the cute cheeks in front of him, rubbing in more cream to ease the pain and the stiffness.

"Open your legs, boy, I'm going to put a little cream inside as well. You aren't split, and it will not be sore for long."

The finger sliding inside him gave him an instant erection, which made him blush. Sky noticed, and told him to turn over. Reluctantly, Matt rolled over to reveal a very pretty penis, uncut, straight, and quite thick.

Sky rolled the foreskin back and, leaning forward, kissed the head softly, making Matt gasp and Sky laugh.

"Did you like that, boy?"

Embarrassed, but excited, Matt almost whispered, "Yes, Master."

Leaning forward again, Sky took the whole of the head into his mouth and licked it all over, sucking gently on it, as well. He was watching Matt as he did it, with a wicked twinkle in his eyes.

"How about that, boy?"

"Oh yes, Master." Matt could hardly believe what he had seen.

"You gave me so much sexual pleasure this afternoon, I am going to give you some now. Lay back and relax."

Matt watched as Sky took his penis back into his mouth, sucking it like a baby's pacifier, while using his hands to play with Matt's balls and run the other hand over his chest to play with his nipples. The sensations were all so new, that Matt could not last long, and had a monumental orgasm, spraying the inside of Sky's mouth with jet after jet of boy juice. Sky was grinning, and Matt was panting when it was over, and Sky slid up the bed to kiss the boy gently on the lips.

"You are one very sweet boy, Matt. I hope you enjoyed that."

Eyes open like saucers, Matt could only nod.

"Go and shower; there is a complete outfit in the wardrobe. Put it on and join me for dinner."

Sky left a very contented young man then, even more confused than he was before. When he had showered, Matt opened the wardrobe and found a shelf with a pair of mini briefs on it, and a watch. Hanging was a silk collarless shirt and a pair of fine cotton trousers.

The shirt was deep maroon and the trousers powder blue; for his feet there was a pair of powder blue suede sandals to match his trousers. He brushed his hair and looked in the full length mirror before going to find Sky. He covered his ears with his hands to see what he would look like without the dangling lobes, and liked what he saw.

I must have been mad to disfigure myself like that, was his thought, and he was suddenly looking forward to tomorrow when plastic surgery would restore his ears to normal.

He found Sky in a formal dining room, with candles lighting the whole room. He sat where he was told, and immediately opened the conversation.

"Will my ears really be as good as new tomorrow after the plastic surgery, Master?"

Sky looked at him seriously, and said, "What did I tell you about talking, boy?"

Matt blushed, dropped his eyes, and said, "I'm sorry, Master; please forgive me."

"I think I might, if you tell me why you asked the question."

Blushing furiously, Matt said, "I realized, looking in the mirror after I had dressed, how much nicer I look when I am normal."

Sky clapped. "Bravo; well said, Boy; I'm proud of you. What about those tattoos?"

Feeling a little more confidant, Matt looked at Sky and said, "I am sure I will look better without those as well, Master; but please, may I keep one special one?"

"What special one?"

Matt undid his shirt and slipped it off his right shoulder, "That one, Master," he said, pointing to a small angel and the word *mother* tattooed underneath.

Sky nodded, "Your mother is dead isn't she, Matt?"

The boy nodded, and produced a small tear.

"That was when you started to go off the rails wasn't it?"

"Yes, Master. I missed her so much."

"Well, we had better get you sorted then, so that if she is watching you she can be proud of you."

That was too much for Matt; he realized what a fool he had been, and just burst into tears.

"I'm sorry, Master, I have been such a fool."

"That's true, but we will get it right before we send you home, hopefully without too many painful sessions like this afternoon."

Matt's sense of humor came through then. "Oh it wasn't all painful, Master." They looked at each other then, and both burst out laughing.

Dinner was a complete success, and both men went to bed that night, content with what had been achieved.

Part 2
Matt Learns the Highs and Lows of his Existence

The good feelings of the night before dissipated quickly the next morning. Showered, shampooed and shaved, dressed in shorts and T-shirt, Matt was greeted at breakfast by the news that Sky would be leaving him in Alexander's hands for a week.

"I have to go to Spain for the week, Matt; I will be back in about seven or eight days. Obey Alex the same as you would me. He will get you started on the gym programme and watch your swimming every day. I am sure he will time you and expect improvements. Your ears will have to be protected, of course, both for showering and swimming, but the doctor will brief Alex on the requirements. Remember, I expect to hear good things about you on my return, particularly the respect you show Alex. Whatever he asks you to do, you do it with a good attitude, and always with a 'yes, Sir', where appropriate. Don't let me down. I want to see a pretty pale bottom when I return; not a black and blue one."

"Yes, Master."

Matt was disappointed to be losing Sky for the week, but was determined to be a model student. Alex, however, had other ideas. He had noted how quickly Sky had taken to the boy, and, although he would never have admitted it, he was jealous. There was no doubt the boy was quite pretty, and would get more so. He was also quite subservient, which Alex knew Sky liked.

As soon as Sky left, Alex started.

"Hospital now, Boy, but when we return you will immediately disrobe. For the remainder of this week, you will be naked in this house and on the grounds. We have a female housekeeper and two male workers. You will call the woman 'Ma'am' and the men 'Sir.' You will also not cover yourself in a false show of modesty if you see them during the day. All three have very limited English, but I can speak Arabic. So if you disobey me, I will know."

Matt was very unhappy with these instructions but just replied, "Yes, Sir."

The hospital was interesting; more a private clinic really. When he left, his ears were enclosed in bandages and hard plastic shields. He had a special waterproof cap that he was told to wear while swimming or showering, and to return every two days to have the work inspected and the dressing changed. At the house, he immediately disrobed and reported to Alex.

Matt was like a little boy at the thought of being normal again physically. Unfortunately, Alex was not as enthusiastic, and managed to deflate Matt in consequence. He had to sunbathe in his Speedos for an hour, but was allowed to rest for the remainder of the day. Dinner was a somber affair taken by the pool, and Matt was subjected to the scrutiny of the staff in his naked state. Alex appeared to be going out of his way to embarrass him. He was made to get up from the table and bend over to pick up Alex's napkin in front of the waiter; then reach up to readjust the position of a lamp, thereby ensuring a very obvious full frontal view for the same waiter. Early to bed, but Matt didn't mind; he was excited about the next day and seeing how his skin would look without the tattoos.

It was not until the third day that Alex started. The dressings had been changed, skin was free of tattoos, except the little angel, and Matt was obviously in high spirits.

"I want you to do your fifty laps; I will time you."

Matt loved to swim, so no problem. When he finished, Alex noted the time, and then sent him off to shower. When Matt came back, the housekeeper was talking to Alex. He said something to her in Arabic, and she stepped back, looking at Matt.

"Have you cleaned yourself properly, boy?"

Matt felt affronted.

"Of course I have."

"Sir."

Matt cursed himself.

"Sorry, Sir."

"Let me see. Turn round, bend over and pull your cheeks apart; we'll start the inspection there."

Matt blanched. "Can the housekeeper leave please, Sir?"

"No, do it."

Tears of embarrassment coursed down Matt's face, as he turned and complied with Alex's instruction. He felt a finger run down the crack of his bottom and worry his rosebud.

"Stand up, turn round, boy. Smell that."

He offered up the finger he had used to worry Matt.

Matt did.

"Does it smell?"

"No, Sir." Matt replied, still crying with embarrassment.

"Lick it, and tell me if it tastes."

Matt wanted to throw up, but did it.

"No, Sir."

"Same position then."

The action was repeated, but this time Alex pushed a finger completely into Matt, eliciting a cry of anguish, knowing the housekeeper was watching. Alex pulled it out, then used both hands to spread Matt's cheeks as wide as he could before releasing them and pushing two fingers in to his anus, rotating them, and fucking him with them for a minute. Matt was quite distraught by this time. He turned round again and was told to lick the fingers clean. That was too much. Matt collapsed in front of Alex, crying and begging not to do it.

"Do it or you get the cane."

Matt couldn't.

"I won't; that is disgusting! I won't do it! You will have to kill me first!"

"Very well, you know your way to the punishment room; go."

Once in the room, Matt had time to look around. There was a rack of canes, a selection of restraints in a basket, the bench, a body sling, (Matt had seen one once in a sex magazine), a selection of butt plugs on a shelf, and a pair of dildos laying on the bench. He didn't like any of it.

"After this lesson, boy, I doubt you will refuse to obey me again." Alex picked up wrist restraints and put them on Matt, (this pair had about eighteen inches of chain between them); ankle restraints were next, with no chain; a cock gag was third.

"I don't want to hear you screaming, so you can suck on that to practice for the real thing when I am ready."

Matt knew now that he was going to be hurt, and started to shake. Alex laid him on the bench on his back, strapped him down at his chest as before, and then pulled his legs up one at a time, clipping the wrist restraints to the ankle ones. The final piece of equipment was a four foot wide bar that the restraints were clipped to, thereby spreading Matt wide and uncomfortable. Alex walked over and picked up a cane, walked back to Matt and, with no preamble, just struck out, catching him on the upper legs. The pain was unbelievable, making Matt choke before he lost consciousness.

He came back to consciousness slowly, still choking and sobbing and Alex did it again, if anything harder than before. When he regained consciousness, he could feel the blood running down his bottom. The pain was unbelievable! Alex looked at him and picked up the largest of the dildos. He pushed it straight into Matt until the balls on the end stopped further penetration; he immediately delivered two very hard strokes to each side of the dildo, catching the cheeks and the back of the thighs.

When he regained consciousness this time, there was no gag. He found out later that he had been choking to death on his own vomit, so Alex had removed it. He could see the blood running down both thighs.

"Wash your mouth out and then you can suck me for a while."

Matt did as he was told, watching Alex all the time. He stripped completely, and when he turned to face Matt, Matt's eyes nearly shot out of his head. Alex had an enormous penis; very long and thick.

"Now suck on this, boy; excite me with your mouth and tongue."

Matt did his best, but he was very inexperienced, and still in considerable pain.

Ten minutes of licking and slurping on Alex had achieved nothing except to get the cock very wet.

"Lousy blowjob, Boy. Let's see if your ass can do any better."

The dildo was pulled out and, with just a little extra spit, Alex shoved his penis in. Matt screamed, and didn't stop until he passed out again. Alex just fucked him to orgasm and left him.

Matt woke in more pain than he had ever known, inside and out. It was dark, and he had no idea how long he had been unconscious. He lay there for what seemed hours, fighting the pain and wondering how long this nightmare was going to last. Who had organised his abduction? Did they know what he was being subjected to? He wanted to go home and apologize to his dad; get a job; and make his father proud of him, and his mother, too.

The lights went on, and the male helper came in, looked at Matt's rear end, and gasped. He ran out and came back with a first aid kit and a bowl of warm water. He gently swabbed the blood away, and gasped again. Alex had split him quite badly; plus, the cane had been wielded so hard that the strokes had also drawn blood. Totally cleaned up and dried, the helper applied lots of antiseptic cream to stop infection, and helped Matt to his bedroom. Once in bed, he made him take painkillers, before covering him with a light sheet. The last thing he did, before going to bed himself, was to telephone Sky and tell him what he had found in the punishment room.

The next morning, Alex tried to get Matt out of bed, but the boy was unable to move under his own power. Alex struck his bottom with his bare hand, and Matt was unconscious again. When he came to again, he just lay where he was and cried. He was in the depths of a depression that he believed could only get worse.

He slept again, but vaguely felt someone stroking his bottom again, and sliding a finger gently into him. His comfort level increased again, and he slept more. When he woke again, it was getting dark, and his disorientation increased. He was still in considerable pain, but he finally came to full awareness, and tried to get out of bed. He screamed with the pain, but continued; he had to pee; it was desperate. The acute pain caused him to vomit as he peed, and he cried with the pain and discomfort. He washed out his mouth, and staggered back to bed. He didn't make it; Sky caught him, as he was leaving the bathroom, before he hit the floor in another faint, and held him close.

"I'm so sorry, Baby. I had no idea Alex resented you so much."

The feeling of safety was too much, and Matt broke down completely, passing out again. He woke several times during the night, and every time, Sky was there to administer another load of treatment. It was three days before Matt fully joined the world. Sky had fed him broth and juices, high protein drinks, and lots of bottom treatments during his conscious spells. Now he was fully aware, and cried softly as Sky held him.

"I won't allow anyone to hurt you again, Baby. Get well soon, so that I can show you how much I have come to love you."

Matt wasn't sure he had heard correctly, but he didn't care; he felt safe, and that was all that mattered.

By the time he was able to move around freely, his ears were healed; the raw skin from the laser removal of his tattoos was gone. He had a slight limp, as he walked alongside the pool to join Sky for breakfast. Sky looked at the boy as he approached, and winced. He had aged, and he blamed himself.

"Come and sit here, Boy; the seat has plenty of padding."

"Thank you, Master."

The voice was weak, the eyes haunted, the skin pale; Sky wanted to weep.

"Matt, I am going to make you a promise today. I am going to bring you back to full health and mobility, fitness and looks, before I send you home. Anything you want that I can give you, I will." Matt believed him; Sky looked so contrite and sounded so sincere.

After breakfast, Sky helped him to get naked, and he sunbathed for a while. Sky winced when he looked at the cane weal's that were still quite inflamed with scabbing across the length of them. The skin had been broken, because of the ferocity of the strokes. There was a little nerve and tissue damage, which would take time to heal. He parted Matt's legs and pulled his cheeks apart to look at his anus.

"Well, the inside is healing nicely, boy. We will have you well before you know it."

"Thank you, Master, but why did Alex do it? Why did he hate me so much?"

"I'm sorry, Matt; he was jealous of the affection I started to show you. I didn't know he loved me."

Matt wondered about this, as he soaked up the sun. Did Sky love him? If so, was Sky gay? He had felt incredible sensations when Sky had fucked him; did that make him gay as well? Would he like Sky as a lover? That was the question that, when he answered it, answered others. He would love to have Sky as a lover; he admired him; he thought he was sexy; most important, he felt safe with Sky, now.

"Permission to speak, Master?" Sky dropped down beside Matt and ran a hand over his back and buttocks.

"You don't have to ask permission any more, boy, and you call me Sky in the future."

"Are you gay, Sky?"

"Yes, Boy."

"Are you in love with me?"

"Yes, I think so."

Matt thought about this, until Sky told him it was time to tan his front. He turned over, and watched as Sky started to rub in sun block. He coated his whole body, leaving his tackle until last. Sky watched Matt's eyes, as he took hold of his penis and rubbed in the cream. Matt loved it, and closed his eyes. For the first time since his trauma, Matt felt a stirring in his member.

As he came to full erection, he said, "Oh, Sky, that feels so good."

"Mmm, I agree, boy; it feels very good to me as well."

Sky slowly jacked Matt to an orgasm; nothing heavy, just some gentle caressing and slow jerking of his cock. He felt a contented sigh of appreciation as he orgasmed, and Sky leant forward to kiss Matt on the lips.

"Thank you, Sky; I feel safe with you. Are you going to look after me for a long time?"

"Unfortunately not; but if my love for you continues to grow, can I visit you in England?" For some reason, this answer upset Matt. He realized he wanted to remain here for a long time.

"Will you kiss me again, Sky? I think I like you kissing me."

Sky laughed. "That's good, because I enjoy kissing you as well."

It was several weeks later that Sky watched Matt walking alongside the pool with no limp. He stood up and took the boy in his arms.

"Your limp has gone completely, Matt. I am so pleased. Now you are completely well. The lines of the cane are almost gone as well. You look more beautiful than ever; can I make love to you today?"

Matt looked surprised, but so pleased.

quite unintentionally, Sky started to pee. He stopped as quickly as he could get control of his bladder; but, in that time, Matt had taken several mouthfuls, which he had swallowed.

"Oh, Baby, I am so sorry; I didn't mean to do that!"

Matt was wide eyed, realizing what he had done, and knew that he didn't mind. It was part of his lover, and that had to be alright. He slid back up the bed and snuggled into Sky's chest, kissing it softly.

"It's ok; I don't mind. I love you, Sky; you can do anything you like to me."

HOW DIFFERENT this job for his boss had turned out compared to all the others. He had never got involved physically with a problem. Alex had been the recipient of his love juice when he was horny, but he had never come close to guessing that it was more than just a quick fuck to Alex. Matt was the one he had not looked for; too many complications; but this boy was divine and so loving; it was almost frightening.

When he could think of no more excuses for keeping Matt in the villa, he knew he was going to fly home with him and ask his boss to let him have Matt as an assistant.

That day, with no work to do, Sky spent the whole day with Matt, just lying around the pool, hitting the gym for a good workout and, of course, doing lots of swimming.

Chilling out on sun beds after lunch, Matt rolled up on one elbow to look at Sky, and said, "Sky, where are we?"

"Morocco, Matt; Mediterranean coast."

"Oh, Dad's boss has a villa out here somewhere, I think." Sky nearly fell off his bed with shock, and Matt picked up on it. He looked shocked, as well, as his brain put two and two together.

"Oh shit; you work for Jack Rushton! I was abducted at his behest, because I had got out of control, and Dad couldn't handle me. Just the kind of thing Jack would do to help an old employee."

"I'm sorry, Matt; you'll never prove it, but I won't lie to you. Yes, what you said is true. Your Dad loves you very much. He told Jack you were all he had left of his wife, but he thought he was going to lose you to drugs. He went to Jack in desperation. I could have let you go home anytime in the last few weeks, but I am truly in love with you, and persuaded Jack to let me keep you here."

Matt's brain was in turmoil. "I need to think, Sky," and with that, he wandered off, still in his naked state. He found a quiet corner of the grounds overlooking the sea, and tried to sort out his feelings. Love for his Dad; however wrong the abduction was, he knew his Dad loved him, and did it for the best. Sky…now that was more complex. Yes, he loved Sky; he felt safe with him now, but the first few days were terrifying and painful. Jack was playing God, and Matt thought that was wrong. But did the end justify the means? He thought about where he was going with his life a few weeks ago, and the answer was, nowhere. Now he looked good, he felt good, he had discovered his sexuality, and a love to go with it. He now had a foundation on which to build his life, instead of the drug-induced quicksand he had left behind.

His brain had now analyzed the situation, his feelings, and his desired course of action. Time to go back to Sky. A very worried man watched Matt approach. As he got closer, Sky could see the determination in his eyes. Matt dropped onto his knees beside Sky, took his face in his hands, and kissed him tenderly on the lips. Pulling back, he said,

"I want to stay here with you Sky, as long as Jack will allow it, but can I telephone my Dad and talk to him tonight? I need to tell him that I love him, and I will be home soon."

Sky nodded, not trusting himself to speak yet; but his eyes told Matt part of what he wanted to know… relief, love…that would do for starters. Eventually, Sky spoke.

"I'll need to clear it with Jack, but I guess the answer will be 'yes.' You really want to stay here with me, Matt?"

"Mmm, I do love you, Sky. It was evil my first few days here, but you turned me round and made me human again and, best of all, you showed me my true self, and fell in love with me as well."

Sky pulled Matt to his feet, kissed him passionately, and said, "Come with me; I'm going to show you just how much I love you."

Matt almost danced alongside Sky to his suite, knowing what was coming, but not having a clue how exquisitely sensual and mind bending it was going to be. Sky didn't so much make love to Matt, that sunny Moroccan afternoon, as take him on a trip to another planet.

Matt couldn't stop crying tears of happiness for nearly half an hour after Sky and he had their last orgasm. He had lost count of how many times Sky had made him cum; all he knew was that, after each one, he loved this man more. He soaked Sky's bed in happy tears before falling asleep.

Dinner was a quiet affair by the pool. About the only thing said, apart from talking to the waiter, was Matt's comment, "You really do love me, Sky, don't you?"

"Yes, Boy; more than I ever dreamt I would."

"I know; no one could have made love to me like you did this afternoon just out of lust."

Matt's conversation with his Father was short that night but it contained all the essential ingredients.

"HELLO, DAD, this is Matthew; how are you?"

"I'm fine son; missing you, but I understand you are safe."

"Yes, Dad. I am not only safe, but very well. I am very fit, have a great tan, and will be home soon. What I really rang for tonight, Dad, was to tell you that I love you, and I'm sorry I went off the rails. I guess I really missed Mum more than I could tell you."

"I know; I guess we both needed each other, and neither of us could say it. We'll change all that when you get home. Look after yourself, son. I love you, too. Goodnight and sweet dreams."

"Thanks, Dad. Goodnight."

THERE WAS a problem for both of them now. Matt wanted to go home to see his Dad, but he wanted Sky as well. Sky didn't want to let him go home, in case they were parted semi permanently. Sky talked to Jack the next day, and came clean.

"Jack, I like this job, and I know you think I do it ok, but you have to know now I am gay, and I have fallen in love with young Matt. It's reciprocated, so no problem. The problem is that we want to be together. So, two possible solutions: I resign and try to find a job near Matt's home, or you employ Matt as my assistant to replace Alex. If you choose the latter, I'll teach him all he needs to know."

"Provisionally, Sky, the latter case, but we'll talk together when you bring Matt home. When do you intend doing that?"

"We'll come home next weekend, Jack, and be in your office on Monday morning."

Nothing could have worked out better. Sky stayed in the company flat, while Matt went home and told his Dad everything that had happened to him.

"I'm sorry you aren't going to have any grandchildren, Dad, but I love Sky so much. I know he is where I want to be for the rest of my life."

"I love you, Matt. There is so much of your mother in you; we have both been fools. I'll not abandon you for being gay; just make sure you aren't a stranger. And I'd like to meet the man who has stolen my son's heart, and is about to take him off to Spain and Morocco, I understand." There was a twinkle in Mark's eyes as he said it, and Matt gasped.

"How did you know, Dad?"

"Jack discussed it with me when Sky had told him. He was going to veto it, until he talked to me, and I told him it was your life, and I wanted to be a part of it, but not the controller of it. Go and find your Sky son, and your happiness."

Matt hugged his Dad and cried as he said, "Thank you, Dad. I've been such a fool, but I've found love because of it. I'll try to make you proud of me; I promise."

"I know you will, boy."

JACK INTERVIEWED Matt on the Monday, with Sky present. He could see the love Matt had for Sky every time he looked in his direction, so he made his decision on that basis.

"I'm going to turn you over to, Sky, Matt; he will complete your education, and on your 21st birthday, I expect you to be ready to be appointed Assistant Property Manager for my company. Don't let me down, and, more importantly, don't let your Dad down. We both have faith in you; and I know, despite his love for you, Sky will not let you slack."

Matt just about floated out of Jack's office, he was so happy! Sky brought him back to earth.

"Back to my flat, Matt; we need to have a serious talk." A little shock treatment is how a casual observer would have classified the next half hour.

"During the next two years, Matt, you will have a series of exams to sit. Failing any of them is not an option, so your regime will be fairly rigid for studying. I know at times it will become tedious, but you must keep at it. If you slack at all, I will punish you. I love you, Matt, but corporal punishment is a natural part of my life, so you will be subject to it where necessary. Do you understand?"

"Yes, Sky. I will work hard to make you proud of me. Will you use the cane on me like you did before?"

"If I have to, yes, but I much prefer the paddle; painful, but not destructive. I want to make love to your beautiful bottom every day; not be coating it in cream to bring out the bruising."

Matt hopped into his lap. "Mmm, I will be very, very good. I don't want my sadistic lover to appear ever." A loving kiss and Sky had to laugh.

"I will find it very hard to punish you if you are bad, Matt, but I will do it if necessary."

Part 3
<u>Matt's New World</u>

England was a whirl of activity for Matt. He needed new clothes for his job, and all the books for his course in property management, plus a couple of weeks with a special tutor to get him started in the right direction, and the compilation of a study and interim examination program. By the time he had finished, he felt he needed a holiday. On the family front, Sky had met Mark and been approved. He had also moved in with Matt.

"I'm not going to have you here for long, boy and, I know you will want to be with Sky, so it will be easier and more convenient if he stays with you."

Life could not have been better for Matt. He saw the boys from the band he had been with, and realized what losers they were, doing just enough work to fund their drug habits. He had Sky's love and, at last, the love and respect of his father.

"I promise I'll make you proud of me, Dad, and I'll never fear Mum looking down on me to see what I'm up to."

The cuddles had come at last, and neither man felt embarrassed at the closeness and affection that both had always felt, but never been able to express.

"Time to go home, boy; we have work to do." There was a tearful goodbye and the promise of frequent visits.

MOROCCO WAS hot, but clothes shed, and it didn't matter. Brief shorts, Speedos or nothing was the dress code most of the time.

Matt settled down to his studies, usually carried out at a table in the shade by the pool. Two three-hour sessions per day was Sky's regimen for him.

"Fits in perfectly with your computer battery life, Matt. The remainder of the day you can work and relax with me. We are going to keep the body in good shape, as well as the mind."

They flew to Spain occasionally, for business, with Matt soaking up the knowledge that came out of these trips. A few trips were made to Marina Smir, a little way along the coast where Jack was funding a development within the marina. On their first trip, Sky explained,

"We'll go and see it one day, Matt, but what we are doing here is trying to emulate The Garden Marina project in Gibraltar; water front restaurants and boutiques, with stylish apartments above. This is a jointly funded project. A British consortium, of which Jack and a chap called Robert Maitland are major players, and the Marina Smir owners."

The next activity that had Matt goggle eyed was a similar case to himself. Sky had gone to pick up another bad lad from another of Jack's companies.

"You'll meet him at breakfast, Matt." Sky briefed Matt, in bed, on his return from picking up the boy. "Not quite a mirror image of your case, but this one is going off the rails, and is already eighteen having dropped out for two years so he only had GCSEs. I hope we are going to be able to send him back very quickly to do his 'A' Levels without losing a term."

Matt was fascinated the next morning. He took Alex's role and went to wake the boy up.

"Jamie, good morning. My name is Matt, but while you are here you are to call me Sir."

"Fuck off; I don't know who you are or what you've done to me, but I'll see you in hell before I call you Sir! Fuck, you only look the same age as me."

"Whatever, I will be back to collect you in 15 minutes. The Master wants you showered, shaved and teeth cleaned. I suggest you comply; it is very painful when you don't."

Fifteen minutes later, Jamie was still unwashed and crashed on his bed. Matt just shrugged. "I'll be back at one o clock to take you to lunch, if you are showered, shaved and ready to go."

"What about my breakfast?"

"You aren't ready, so I won't be taking you."

By lunch time and Jamie was ready. Sky had to get heavy to get any compliance, and Matt winced. Spanked very hard twice and, with a very sore bottom, Jamie sat down for lunch.

"You have an interim exam, next week don't you, Matt?"

"Mmm, Jack is sending an invigilator to conduct it."

"Confident?"

"Well, I've kept up my study schedule, so I should be ok."

"Don't think I'll need the paddle then?"

Matt looked a little shocked. "Would you really, Sky?"

"I told you I would, and I will. If you have any problems, I can help."

"Thanks."

"Now, Jamie, let me tell you what is going to happen to you. We are going to get you physically fit, give you a nice tan, and get you back into the study mode, ready to go home and join your 'A' Level class. Compliance with my instructions means pleasure. Disobey me and that means pain. If you want to know how much pain, ask Matt how many weeks it took for him to walk properly after his last punishment."

"Ugh, don't remind me, Sky. I thought I was going to die that night." Jamie didn't know whether this was a wind up or not, but he was still very belligerent.

"Ok, Boy, what bullshit are you going to spin me?"

Quick as a flash, Sky had him in an arm lock, and marched him off to the punishment room, with Matt following. He was restrained over the whipping bench, the same as Matt had been. His arse was already blushing from his spanking, but Sky was brutal, rendering him unconscious with ten strokes of the cane.

The assault with the cane looked frightening. Jamie was pleading, begging, and sobbing from the first one, and was barely conscious by the tenth one. Matt suddenly realized that Sky had not broken the skin, unlike Alex did with him.

"Look after him, Matt. Take him back to his room and treat him, and we'll talk to him again at dinner time."

"**I'M GOING** to kill that bastard, Boy, as soon as I can," was Jamie's greeting to Matt when he went to fetch him to dinner.

"Fine. I'm Sir, and if you call me 'boy' again, I'll give you ten with the cane, as well. Now get your naked arse down to the pool."

Matt could now see clearly where Sky was coming from with *his* early treatment; disrespect rankled. By the time he went to bed that night, Jamie had received a total of twenty slaps barehanded and twenty with the cane. He was very uncomfortable, but being a slow learner, he wasn't finished yet. Ten before breakfast for not calling Matt "Sir" and ten after breakfast for not calling Sky "Master". By lunch time, he was very sore and barely able to walk. He was also beginning to realize life was not going to get better unless he changed his attitude.

During the course of the next seven days, Jamie was not allowed any clothes, and he was systematically humiliated in front of the staff, particularly the housekeeper. The scene that had Matt almost peeing himself, in his attempts not to laugh, was only carried out once, and was so similar to his own experience with Alex he almost sympathized with Jamie, but not quite.

All three had been for a workout in the gym and then gone to shower in their own bathrooms. When Jamie appeared at the pool afterwards, Matt and Sky were there, clad in shorts and polo's, to emphasize Jamie's nudity. The housekeeper was there talking to Sky. As Jamie approached, she stood back, and Jamie looked embarrassed and covered his genitals.

"Walk straight, Boy; swing your arms properly; be proud of who you are." He stopped in front of Sky, still blushing, and moved his hands to cover his private parts again.

"Stand up straight, Boy; spread your legs and grip your hands behind your head." Reluctantly, Jamie did.

"Are you clean, Boy?"

"Yes, Master," was the surly reply. Sky lifted Jamie's cock, making him jump back.

"If you move again without instruction, I will whip you unconscious."

Sky did the same thing; and, this time, Jamie didn't move. With his other hand, Sky stroked Jamie's balls and sniffed his hand. Then he skinned Jamie's cock and ran a saliva slicked finger round the glans. With a sharp intake of breath, and Jamie started to get hard. Sky continued caressing Jamie's balls and stroking his glans, until he was fully erect. Then he stroked the length of the shaft before releasing it, smelling his fingers again, and, looking into Jamie's eyes, smiled and said,

"Very pretty, Boy. Now turn round and spread your legs wider." Jamie looked frightened, but complied.

"Now bend over and grip your ankles. Mrs. Moreno, please come here and spread his cheeks a little more for me." Sky guessed that would be too much, and grabbed Jamie's hips as he tried to get away.

"Stay where you are." And that was accompanied by two very hard slaps that made Jamie squeal.

Humiliation resumed, and Sky buried two fingers in Jamie, fucking him with them for a couple of minutes before walking round in front of him and making him lick them.

"Stand up, boy, and tell me, did the fingers taste of anything?"

"Just a little soapy, Master," was Jamie's tearful reply.

"Good Boy. Would you like me to check you for cleanliness every day after gym, with Mrs Moreno present?

"No, Master; please don't."

"Ah, *please* is in your vocabulary. You may go back to your room now and dress in the clothes on your bed, before returning here to join us for lunch."

The psychology was perfect: total humiliation, followed five minutes later by clothes and friendliness.

"I think we will all sunbathe naked for an hour after lunch, and then Jamie and I will swim, Matt, and you will study."

The routine was established then. Matt studied in the mornings, while Sky explained to Jamie what was expected of him here, and in the future at home. He was allowed a siesta, the same as Matt, in the worst heat of the afternoon, but Sky usually went off somewhere without Matt knowing where.

Late afternoon, Matt would normally go down to the pool for a swim, but on this particular day stopped by Jamie's room to ask him to join him. Both boys were surprised when Matt walked in, because Jamie was finger fucking himself while jacking off. Jamie had his eyes closed, so he didn't realize Matt was there, until he felt a soft hand caressing his nipples and Matt's voice saying, "I would be delighted to put my penis where your fingers are, if you would like." Jamie nearly jumped off the bed with shock. He immediately burst into tears when he realized Matt had seen everything.

"Please don't tell, Sky; he'll beat me."

"No, he won't Jamie; he might beat me if I were to put my cock where your fingers were, but I doubt that as well."

"Are you gay then, Matt?"

"Mmm, I found out when I was in your position here in this villa."

"And Sky doesn't mind?"

"No, Jamie, Sky doesn't mind. Is being gay part of the reason your behavior is so rotten?"

"Yeah, I guess so. By being a hard arse, I hope to keep my sexuality a secret. No one at home would understand."

"I'll talk to Sky; I'm sure he'll have a solution for that."

"Please, Matt, don't tell him."

"Of course I'm going to tell him; we both want to see you back with your family, so he needs to know all the facts."

"My family will hate me if they find out, and my step father will disown me; he's a pig."

"Well we can't do anything about that at the moment. Would you like to come for a swim with me; Sky is still away."

The two boys had a good swim and were horsing around in the water when Sky got back. He watched them for a while and guessed what Matt now already knew. At dinner he brought up the subject.

"Jamie, if your family disowned you because you are gay, but we found another loving home for you where they knew, would that be acceptable to you?"

Jamie was almost speechless. "How did you know? Matt told you, yes?"

"No, but I saw you playing this afternoon, and it clicked. Have you made love to him yet, Matt?"

"Oh no, Sky."

"But you would like to."

Matt blushed and looked down; he couldn't look Sky in the eyes.

"It's alright, lover. You know how much I love you, but a romp with Jamie isn't going to damage that love."

Jamie was fast reaching mental overload with all this conversation. Almost in shock he said,

"You two are lovers?"

"Yes, Jamie. Matt was like you when he came here, and I fell in love with him after we had straightened him out."

"Wow that is awesome! Will you fall in love with me if I'm good?" Matt and Sky laughed, and Sky jumped up to grab Jamie in a hug.

"I don't think so, Jamie; but I am sure, if you want it, Matt will make love to you while we sort out your life."

Jamie looked at Matt and said very softly, and with half closed eye lids, "I think I would like that, Master." Jamie told Sky everything then, most of it centering on his abusive stepfather.

Sky talked to Jack that night, and found out that it was Jamie's mother who had gone to him; she was a long serving employee, the same as Matt's father, but the new husband didn't like Jamie, and would use his homosexuality as an excuse to throw him out.

"Jamie's problem won't be solved, Jack, unless we can place him somewhere, with someone, who will love him whatever he is." The problem was solved a few days later, but more of that in a little while.

BREAKFAST THE next morning.

"I have to go to Spain tomorrow, Matt, for a meeting with Robert Maitland about the Marina project. We can't leave Jamie by himself, and your invigilator will be here in two days, as well. So you are staying. I will be back in four days maximum, at which time I expect Jamie to have continued his regimen, and you to have passed your exam with flying colors. It would be very embarrassing for you if I had to punish you in front of Jamie." Jamie was intrigued and, as soon as he could talk to Matt out of Sky's earshot, he asked him.

"What's with this punishment thing?"

"Sky is my lover, but he is also my mentor and my boss. He won't allow me to slack off because, in two years, I have to be able to qualify as a property manager, or he will lose me. He loves me very much, but that is why he will paddle me if my exam results aren't all he expects."

"And you will let him?"

"Yes, because I love him very much, and want to be with him forever."

"Wow," and that was it.

The next day Sky left and, at siesta time, Matt took Jamie to bed. He wasn't a cute 18-year-old, but he was very well put together, with a sturdy body, a little sloppy, but improving fast; short cropped brown hair; wide spaced green eyes; and a square jaw. He looked older than Matt, and was bigger, but nowhere near as confidant; so it was easy for Matt to dominate, even though he had never fucked a boy before.

It started before they even got to the bedroom. Jamie caught Matt at the top of the stairs, pulled his trousers and pants down, before going down on him. Matt smiled down at his new friend, and stroked his hair.

"Come on, eager beaver; let's get comfortable in bed. We have plenty of time."

Lying together on Jamie's bed, Matt took the lead. This was a new experience for him. Sky always made love to him, but now he was using all Sky's techniques on Jamie. He found it very pleasant to pleasure another body; of course he had blown Sky, so doing it to Jamie was old hat; but not for Jamie who, was amazed at how sensuous it all was.

"Oh gosh, Matt; that is marvelous! Will you promise to do that to me every day?"

Both boys laughed, and Matt continued. He opened Jamie up with well-slicked fingers, until both of them wanted the final act. Matt entered Jamie very gently, stopping as soon as he was over the sphincter, to give Jamie the chance to adjust, and then feeding him his full length.

"Oh, Matt; that feels so good! I can feel every inch of you."

Matt was truly amazed; he had never had feelings like this. He now knew why Sky's orgasms were so intense; and, a few minutes later, he experienced it for himself. Both boys cried with the intensity of their orgasms, and then giggled like a couple of school boys, as they recovered.

"Jamie, one day a boy is going to be very lucky and call you his boyfriend; that was marvelous." Jamie preened.

"Now we have a little problem. I don't want to discipline you, now that we have made love; so you have to be very good from now on, and show Sky the proper respect. You must also work very hard for him, whatever he asks of you. I will ask him if you can call me 'Matt.' After all, we are the same age, and lovers now. So Sir sounds silly."

"Thank you, Matt. I'll try really hard, but what am I doing all this for? I will still have to go back to my family and be something I'm not."

"I doubt that; Sky has a way of making things happen to his satisfaction."

Life took on its regimented role for the next few days, with one downward spike. Matt's examination results were disappointing. This was his first exam for some time, and he wasn't prepared for it. He knew he would do better next time, and he hoped that would be good enough for Sky; but in his heart, he knew it wouldn't. You got punished for what you had done; not rewarded for what you might do.

On Sky's return, Jamie witnessed something that held him in awe of Sky forever. Sat by the pool in the late afternoon sun, Sky was going through Matt's exam, and the invigilator's comments. Both Matt and Jamie were on edge.

"Not good enough, Matt. We'll talk about this in a moment. What about you, Jamie; have you been good?"

"Oh yes, Master; Matt will tell you. I have worked out properly every day; sunbathed naked, and swam the required number of lengths. Matt has my time, and every day I have improved. I have also read the sections of the school books that you set me, and I think I can display an adequate knowledge of each subject."

"He has become very articulate, Matt. Have you two talked a lot?"

"Yes, Master. We have been together, talking for hours every day, when we have not been studying." Matt had reverted to 'Master,' because he knew he was going to be punished.

"Why are you calling me 'Master,' Matt?" Matt looked at Jamie first; then blushing furiously and tearing up, he looked at Sky and said,

"I know you are going to punish me for my examination results, even though I passed; and I don't think I can handle my *lover* beating me, but if it is my *Master*, I can accept it."

"Very well; strip, and display in front of me."

Matt did so without hesitation. Sky stroked his body for a few minutes, before starting to concentrate on his bottom and his cock and balls.

"It will be such a shame to bruise this beautiful bottom, and see this straining erection shrink in anticipation of pain, but you have to learn, Matt. Now go to the punishment room and bring me back a paddle; the one with the red handle, I think."

Matt shivered; that one was a monster. It was heavy rubber, and stung wicked. Because of its weight, it also bruised badly, making the recipient squirm in pain for days afterwards.

Jamie looked half in shock when Matt returned, tears coursing silently down his face. He stood in front of Sky again, and passed him the paddle.

"Prostrate yourself over the table, Matt; grip the far edge, spread your legs wide, and push back." It looked incredibly erotic, and Jamie was very quickly completely erect.

"You had better strip as well, Jamie; I have work for your penis after this. Stand behind Matt, Jamie, but clear of my swinging arm."

Sky swung the first one with medium force, still enough for Matt to squirm and grunt in pain. He didn't want to disgrace himself in front of Jamie, but the next one was harder.

"Oh God, Master, that hurt." He sobbed.

The next eight were horrendous! Matt was sure each one was harder than its predecessor. He screamed, he begged, he pleaded with Sky, to no avail. Then came the humiliation. Jamie was still rock hard, so Sky said,

"Fuck him, Jamie; now, and hard!"

Jamie didn't dare disobey Sky. He was terrified of receiving the same treatment, so he powered into Matt until he orgasmed, and then fell forward over Matt's body, apologizing and crying, begging forgiveness.

Sky watched all this and wondered…would his brutality lose him this wonderful boy, because he realized Matt and Jamie had become lovers in his absence. He picked up Matt in his arms and kissed him tenderly.

"I love you so much, Baby, but you have to learn." Matt came back to earth gradually, and realized the brutality of his punishment.

I don't have to take this; I'm not a slave, or in disciplinary rehab like before. I can leave here and go home, were Matt's thoughts. Sky tended to his bruised bottom, and Matt slept.

The next morning, he showed great tenderness and affection towards Jamie, but then turned to Sky and, very simply, with no histrionics, said,

"I want to go back to England, Sky. I don't want to be here anymore. Will you arrange an air ticket for me?" With that, he went back to his room and started to pack.

Jamie found him first. "Are you really going home, Matt?"

"Yes, Jamie. That was brutal punishment yesterday. I don't believe he could do that if he truly loved me."

"What will happen to me now?"

"Behave yourself, and when Sky sends you home, come and live with me and my Dad. You can go to school; and I will, too, to get some more qualifications. I promised my Dad I would make him proud of me, and I will. He knows I am gay, and will accept you as his ward, if I ask him. Oh bugger it! I will go and see Sky now; perhaps he will let you come home with me."

Sky was on the telephone, and Matt could hear him arranging his air ticket, so he interrupted. "Will you order one for Jamie, as well? He is totally rehabilitated, and can come to live with me."

Their eyes met, and Sky nodded, before ordering two tickets for the afternoon flight to Madrid, and onward connection to London. When the deed was done, and Sky looked longingly at Matt. He was too proud to beg, but he did let Matt know his feelings.

"Get undressed, Matt." Matt was so used to doing as Sky told him, that he didn't hesitate.

"Now turn round." Matt did, and heard Sky's sharp intake of breath.

"Remain where you are, Matt; I'll cream your bottom again." As he started to apply the cream, Sky said very softly.

"I'm sorry, Baby; I didn't mean to cause this much damage. I do love you, Matt, and I want you to be proud of what you are becoming."

"I might have taken the punishment, Sky, but making Jamie rape me was too much. We have become tender lovers, so you have damaged Jamie, as well as me. He will be happy living with me, and we will both go back to school. I will make my father proud of me; that was my vow, and I will keep to it." Nothing more was said and, that evening, Matt told his father the reason for his arrival, only leaving out the rape.

"Jamie can stay, Dad, can't he? He is legal to leave his father. You can ask to be his legal guardian until he finishes school, and I will get a job, but continue to study for my Property Management Qualifications in my free time." Mark nodded his agreement and, the next morning, went to see Jack and fill him in on the details.

"I have already talked to Sky, Mark, and he said he went over the top, punishing Matt for his poor exam results. I'll continue to employ Matt if he continues to study, and he can work in the property development department here. He will bump into Sky on occasions, but I can't help that. Tell Matt to come and see me tomorrow, with his study and exam schedule, and we'll see how to fit everything in. Jamie's Mother is happy for Jamie to remain in your household, but would obviously like to see him sometimes."

"That's no problem, Jack. He seems to be a good lad, and he and Matt get on well."

Everything worked out very well. Jamie did go back to school to study for his 'A' levels, and appeared to be happy in this new household. He and Matt improved their friendship, and made love on occasions, but for mutual relief, rather than love. Matt had to admit to Jamie that he missed Sky.

"He was brutal in punishing me, Jamie, and making you rape me; but he was a wonderful lover…so tender and caring. I always felt safe with him."

"I'm glad you are home though, Matt. I like living here with you as my friend. I would find it very frustrating if we didn't have each other to make love to." Matt laughed, and hugged Jamie.

"Me, too; we must be good for each other's sanity."

THE NEXT year flew by, and both Jamie and Matt were pleased with their interim examination results. So was Jack, who had bent over backwards to integrate Matt's study program into a reasonable degree of proper work. He was also amazed at the pass level Matt achieved in every one.

"Matt, how come your first exam, in Morocco, produced such a poor pass?"

"I didn't really know what to expect, Jack. The format was totally different to anything I did at school; but as soon as I clicked on it, the rest was just a matter of studying and soaking up knowledge at work."

"Well, I'm so pleased with you. I want you to go out to Marina Smir for a week. Robert Maitland will be there. I want you to get to know him, because he is my partner in the project. I also want you to become familiar with the Marina Owners. I have plans for you as the project nears completion, and they involve close contact with those two people."

"Thank you, Jack. Will Sky be there as well?"

Jack looked at his young protégé, and wondered aloud,

"Will that worry you, Matt?"

Matt blushed a little. "I don't know, Sir. It is a year since I have seen him. I don't know how I feel about him now."

"Try not to let it worry you. Sky is very important to my organization, and you will need to work with him frequently when you are qualified. I wouldn't want conflict between two such important cogs in my wheel."

Nothing more was said, and Matt went home to think. When he told Jamie, the conversation got very animated.

"Do you think your success this year has been due to the discipline you learnt from Sky?"

Matt was surprised at Jamie's train of thought.

"Mmm, I'm sure it was. I could never study like that when I was at school. I passed my 'A' Levels, but they weren't good passes; not like the exams I have sat this year."

"So lots of loving and a little punishment was good for you?"

"Yeah, I guess. Is this going somewhere, Jamie?"

"I think so, Matt. So the only reason you left Sky was the rape; not the punishment?"

"Sure. I had psyched myself for the punishment, because I know Sky. But it was a bit brutal, and the rape was definitely uncalled for. I passed my exam; just not well enough to please Sky. So, in my opinion he went completely over the top."

"So, do you still love him?"

Jamie looked hard at Matt with that question, and Matt couldn't hold his gaze. Very quietly he said, "Yes, Jamie, I think I still love him. I've missed him this year; he was a wonderful lover. He was always gentle and considerate, and took me to Paradise every time." Realizing what he had said, he took Jamie in his arms and hugged him.

"What we have is good, as well, Jamie; but I love you like a brother, and what we do is great; but Sky was my true love."

"I know that, silly, and I would love to see you and Sky get back together; he is an awesome dude. I also have a confession, Matt; I have found a boyfriend." Matt grinned all over his face.

"That is fantastic, Jamie; tell me about him."

That was it for the two boys. The next hour was total hilarity, as Jamie tried to be serious, and Matt the opposite. Result, Matt realized Jamie was serious about this boy, and was pleased for him.

"I love what we have, Jamie; you are the brother I never had, so I am so pleased for you. I know Dad will be as well. He worries about you finding a lover. I find it quite funny; he talks to me about it sometimes, and I realize he thinks of you as his son now."

Jamie hadn't realized that, so when Mark came in from work, he grabbed him in a hug and said, "Thank you, Dad, for making my life so good. I love you and Matt for being my new family." Mark laughed a little embarrassed laugh.

"Ok, son; what brought that on?"

Jamie blushed, but replied, "Matt and I were talking and I realized all the good things you two have done to make my new life good. I'll try to make you proud of me, the same as Matt does." Mark grabbed both boys in a hug and told them,

"I'm a very lucky man. One year ago, I had one son who I was not very proud of, and was very worried about. Now, I have two wonderful sons to love and be proud of."

There were three pairs of slightly wet eyes as they parted to get ready for dinner.

Part 4
Matt and Sky

During his year with Jack, Matt had learnt to drive, so his instruction for the Marina Smir trip was:

"Fly to Gibraltar, take the ferry to Ceuta in Spanish Morocco, and hire a car. Drive down to Marina Smir, and see what developments are going on along that piece of coast. If anything looks interesting, stop and get all the information you can on it. Don't take more than a couple of days to reach the Marina complex. We'll discuss it when you get back."

Matt thought that sounded fantastic, and the reality was just that. There were a couple of interesting developments, and he was lucky, in both cases, to get to talk to the developers, who both wanted a professional management company to come in and run them when they were complete. With all the details in hand, Matt felt that he had earned his money for this trip.

When he arrived at the Marina, he was shown the apartment allocated to Jack's company; and, once settled in, went looking for Robert Maitland. He tracked his quarry down to the restaurant in the apartment block, and was surprised to see him with an American Indian boy.

[Robert Maitland and Silent Waters are the main characters in my story, "Silent Waters".]

"Good afternoon, Sir; I'm Matthew Stator. I believe you are expecting me."

"Hello, Matthew. I'm pleased to meet Jack's new protégé. I've heard some good things about you." Matt blushed. He had no idea Jack had talked about him, much less that he had sung his praises.

"I would like you to meet my partner, Silent Waters."

Matt was a little flustered. This man was incredibly beautiful, with the most amazing eyes.

"I'm pleased to meet you Silent Waters; Jack didn't tell me Mr. Maitland had a partner."

Silent Waters laughed. "I'm Robert's life partner; nothing to do with business."

"Sit down, Matthew. I'm Robert."

Still a little flustered after Silent Waters revelation, Matt said, "Thank you, Sir."

"May I call you 'Matt, Matthew?"

Matt grinned, as he got his act together. "Yes, Robert, that will be fine."

Matt guessed Robert to be mid thirties, and thought Silent Waters was his age, twenty.

"Silent Waters has been with me for eight years now, Matt, but is not interested in my business; he came with me this week because I needed more crew for the yacht, and he likes this place."

Twenty was obviously way out, was Matt's next thought.

"Robert is going to build us a house here, as part of the development, Matt, so that we can spend more time here. I don't really like sailing, but when we first came here, the yacht was the only good accommodation. Now we use it to please Robert."

Matt saw the look of love that passed between the two, and thought of what might have been with Sky and him.

"Spend the remainder of the day with us, Matt; we'll have dinner on the yacht tonight, and then you and I will look over the development tomorrow. I believe Sky is joining us tomorrow as well, he only has a short drive up the coast from his home. Do you know him, Matt?" Matt blushed again, and mentally kicked himself; he would have to get over this.

"Yes, Robert; Sky was my mentor when I first started in this business."

"Ah, that's good; all friends together, then."

They had lunch together, and then Robert said he had some work to do before meeting the Marina owners at dinnertime. When he left, Silent Waters started.

"You aren't very comfortable with Sky being here tomorrow, are you Matt?" Matt looked like the proverbial deer caught in the headlights.

"You have very expressive eyes. Sky is a very forceful man, isn't he, Matt? Did it all end painfully for you?" Matt looked down before replying.

"Yes, I loved him very much, but he was very cruel to me."

"I'm sorry; I know how destructive that can be. Robert pulled me out of a near suicidal depression, because my previous lover was cruel, as well."

"How old are you, Silent Waters?"

"I'm 26, Matt, and Robert is 37. I am guessing you are 20."

Matt laughed. "Yes, I am. I thought you were, as well, until Robert said you have been together for eight years."

Both young men laughed then.

Matt was seriously impressed with the yacht, when he joined Robert and Silent Waters for dinner with the Marina owner. Robert was very careful to include Matt in all the conversation and fill him in on the detail of the project. By the time the evening was over, he had a very good idea of what he should be looking for the next day. He was determined to impress Sky.

He would have been embarrassed if he had heard the conversation between Robert and Silent Waters that night before they slept.

"YOUNG MATT is a seriously cute kid isn't he Silent Waters?"

"Yes, he is. Do you want to take him to bed?"

Robert laughed, "Mmm, it might be interesting."

"You realize he and Sky were lovers, and Matt left him because he was cruel."

Robert wasn't surprised. "He is a hard man, I know; but I didn't realize he was gay or cruel. I don't think I could hurt Matt; he is delightful." Plenty of room for these two to surprise Matt, but that would depend on how Sky was received.

SKY ARRIVED just after breakfast, and was very surprised to see Matt. They exchanged very perfunctory greetings, before studiously ignoring one another.

The Marina Owner made it clear, as they walked round the complex that he was disappointed with the number of boats using it. There were 283 births, including a half dozen for super yachts; but apart from the owner's super yacht and Robert's seventy foot sailing yacht, there were only five other births occupied. Matt decided to test the waters of his acceptance into this company of seasoned businessmen.

"How much do you charge per foot, Sir, for berths?"

"One US Dollar, Matt."

"And how easily, or how soon, could you have the super market and chandlery operating?"

"Almost instantly; why?"

"Well, an awful lot of live boards, that have been cruising the Med. during the summer, will be looking for winter homes, now that autumn is coming. If you were to halve your berthing fee for long term occupants, and have a well equipped chandlery and supermarket open, you could advertise it, and I am sure you would get a lot of boats for the winter and early spring, who would then return, or at least tell other boats if they had enjoyed it. Perhaps the boat lift could be in operation as well.

I am sure a lot of the boats would want to be lifted before cruising again in the summer." The Owner, Robert and Sky all looked in surprise at Matt, who blushed furiously.

"You could increase your fees again, Sir, when the remainder of the complex is complete, and you would be making money while still building."

"Matt, that makes a lot of sense; I'll get onto that today. Clever boy; I think Jack may have picked a winner with you."

They continued their tour of the complex, discussing the building program, and Sky moved in close to Matt to whisper.

"Well done, boy; I'm proud of you, and so sorry I lost you; it stupid of me. Jack told me how you have excelled in all your exams, and your explanation of why you did so badly your first one."

Matt was overwhelmed at the comments. He never expected Sky to apologize; and why was he so pleased at Sky's praise? Did he still really care?

The remainder of the day went well, with Matt holding his own in discussions with these experienced men. The owner's name was Yusuf, and Matt was pleased to be told to call him by his first name. The discussion then turned to who was going to manage the complex when it was complete.

"When do you qualify, Matt?" came from Robert.

"About one more year, provided I don't fail any exams."

"How would you like to manage this then, Matt?"

Yusuf waved his arm, to take in the whole complex, and Matt gulped.

"This would be an awfully large undertaking for a new boy, Sir."

"It's still Yusuf, Matt, and if you continue to show such maturity and bright ideas, I don't think your age and lack of experience will matter. I am sure Jack will allow Sky to drop in and look things over occasionally, and keep you up to scratch."

Matt was feeling cheeky, so his reply made Sky blush.

"Oh, I'm sure he will, as well, Yusuf; I have experienced Sky's methods of keeping me on my toes." Yusuf, of course, was unaware of the previous relationship, but Robert wasn't, and he laughed raucously.

"Ah, Sky, hoist on your own petard, I believe." he said, grinning widely as he said it.

"Mmm, I didn't realisz what an intelligent and smart young man I had under my wing a year ago. I underestimated him, but I won't ever do that again."

He smiled at Matt as he said it, and it was Matt's turn to blush. All these compliments were making his head spin. Meetings finished for the day, the next round of discussions were set for after lunch the next day. Sky asked Matt if he would like to go back to the villa for dinner and spend the night.

"You would have your own bedroom, Matt. I would just like the opportunity to make small amends for my treatment of you last year. I was very foolish to punish and humiliate you like that. My wishes that you be excellent at your job made me go over the top. Now I can see that excellent is what you are. Jack has kindly kept me informed of your progress. I am so proud of you."

Matt could see that this proud man was trying very hard not to show too much emotion, and failing.

"Do you still love me, then, Sky?"

"Yes, Matt, I still love you."

Typical Sky. No elaboration, just the facts stated, end of story.

"In that case, I would like to have dinner with you. I'll just tell Robert, so that he knows I haven't deserted."

"You really have grown up, haven't you, Matt?"

Matt blushed again, and mentally kicked himself for again letting his pleasure show in this way.

THE VILLA was exactly as Matt remembered it. With autumn approaching, the fierce heat was gone, and he was able to dress for dinner without sweating. They ate by the pool, and Matt realized Sky had made chef pull out all the stops to produce a superb meal. The wines were the best he had ever tasted, the white a very smooth and light Penedes, and the red a heavy, but excellent Rioja. Sky used the time to probe even deeper into Matt's knowledge base, and was amazed at how deep it was.

"You are truly amazing, Matt; who has been teaching you?"

"Thank you, Sky. Jack has taken a personal interest, and allocated senior departmental people to take me under their wing for short period, when particularly interesting activities have been going on."

"Well, it has definitely paid off; and Yusuf's desire to have you run Marina Smir is well founded."

Matt blushed again; praise from this man was incredibly good for his ego and his self-confidence. He knew that the grounding for his success had been made here, and that responsibility for his new life was heavily weighted towards Sky.

"I owe you a great deal for my success, Sky. You turned me round very quickly from a slippery downward spiral to where I am now. I have learnt that success comes from hard work and dedication to the task. I also know, now, that to get respect you have to give respect. My teachers have all helped me enthusiastically, because I show them proper respect for their vastly greater knowledge than my own."

"I am so proud of you. Will you allow me to collect on your debt to me by letting me make love to you tonight?"

Matt looked at Sky in surprise. He would love to say 'yes,' but would this open the flood gates of a love that he had quelled for a year now? Was it possible to resume their affair, or was he going to have his heart broken again if he gave in to his feelings?

"I am flattered, Sky, but don't you think it would be dangerous to open that particular box again?"

"Of course, I do. I would risk it willingly, though, Matt, for the opportunity to start a serious relationship with you again. I have never loved another man before, or since you. What I did was stupid and cruel. No day has passed since you left, when I have not regretted my stupidity."

God, this proud man was opening up his soul tonight! It must have taken a huge amount of courage to reveal his weakness for a failed love. Matt realized this, and felt he would have to risk it as well.

"Yes, Sky, I'll let you make love to me tonight." The loving kiss he received for that comment, took Matt's breath away; he had forgotten how exquisitely Sky kissed.

In the bedroom, Sky started to undress Matt, planting hundreds of tiny kisses on his body as he uncovered it. On his knees, with Matt's crotch only inches from his face, Sky slipped the trousers off before kissing and caressing Matt's inner thighs, and watching his penis grow, until it was rigid. He eased the waist band of his briefs over the cock head, and slid them to the floor, where Matt stepped out of them. Sky kissed one very pretty cock, and then stood up and held Matt at arm's length, while he scanned the whole of his body.

"You are even more beautiful than I remembered, Matt. I think I might disgrace myself making love to you tonight." There was that obvious blush again, and Matt kicked himself. When would he get over this stupidity?

Sky quickly disrobed, before taking Matt back into a warm embrace. The feeling of Sky's hard penis pushing against his tummy made Matt gasp; it felt like a rod of iron.

Lighten it up, or this was going to be spoilt by its intensity, was Matt's thought.

"Mmm, that feels as though you might be pleased to see me in my birthday suit." Matt was grinning as he said it, and Sky, picking up on what Matt was doing, eased the pressure of the hug.

"I guess I've missed you more than I thought." Both relaxed now, and the mood was set for some serious lovemaking. Sky guided Matt over to his bed, and laid him on it in the center.

"Spread your legs wide, Matt, and just relax."

Nothing in Matt's world could come close to the sensations of the next hour. Sky didn't so much make love to Matt, as devour him. His orgasms were so ferocious, and there were so many of them that, eventually, with Sky still inside him, he passed out. The final act, when he regained consciousness, was Sky, who was still inside him, taking him to one more gentle ejaculation in perfect time with his own last one. Too exhausted to get out of bed, both men simply fell asleep, cuddling each other.

When Matt woke, he could hardly move. He was wrapped tight in Sky's embrace, but it was the masses of dried cum, practically gluing their bodies together, that started Matt off giggling. Matt's shaking woke Sky, who realized the same as Matt, and could smell the old sex and dried cum. The result, as he looked into the laughing eyes of his lover, was two almost hysterical but happy men heading for the shower.

"God, you are disgusting, Mr. Stator; how could you sleep like that?" Too much for Matt, he was crying with the combination of happiness, suppressed fun, and love for this man.

The look that Robert gave Silent Waters, the next afternoon said it all. No chance of enjoying Matt's body now was his correct guess. Matt was in love again, big time!

Matt passed his final exams and, with the support of all three major players, became General Manager of Marina Smir. Sky moved into Matt's apartment with him, and worked from there on all of Jack's other projects. The Villa, where it had all started, became a weekend retreat for Matt and Sky, when Matt could afford to be away from the Marina for a whole weekend.

Jamie came out for a holiday, with his boyfriend, after passing his 'A' Levels, and told Matt how he would be off to university in the autumn. Sky took the credit for turning him round, and Matt and Jamie let him; it didn't matter who had achieved it; everyone was just happy that it had happened.

THE END

Here is a sample from another story you may enjoy:

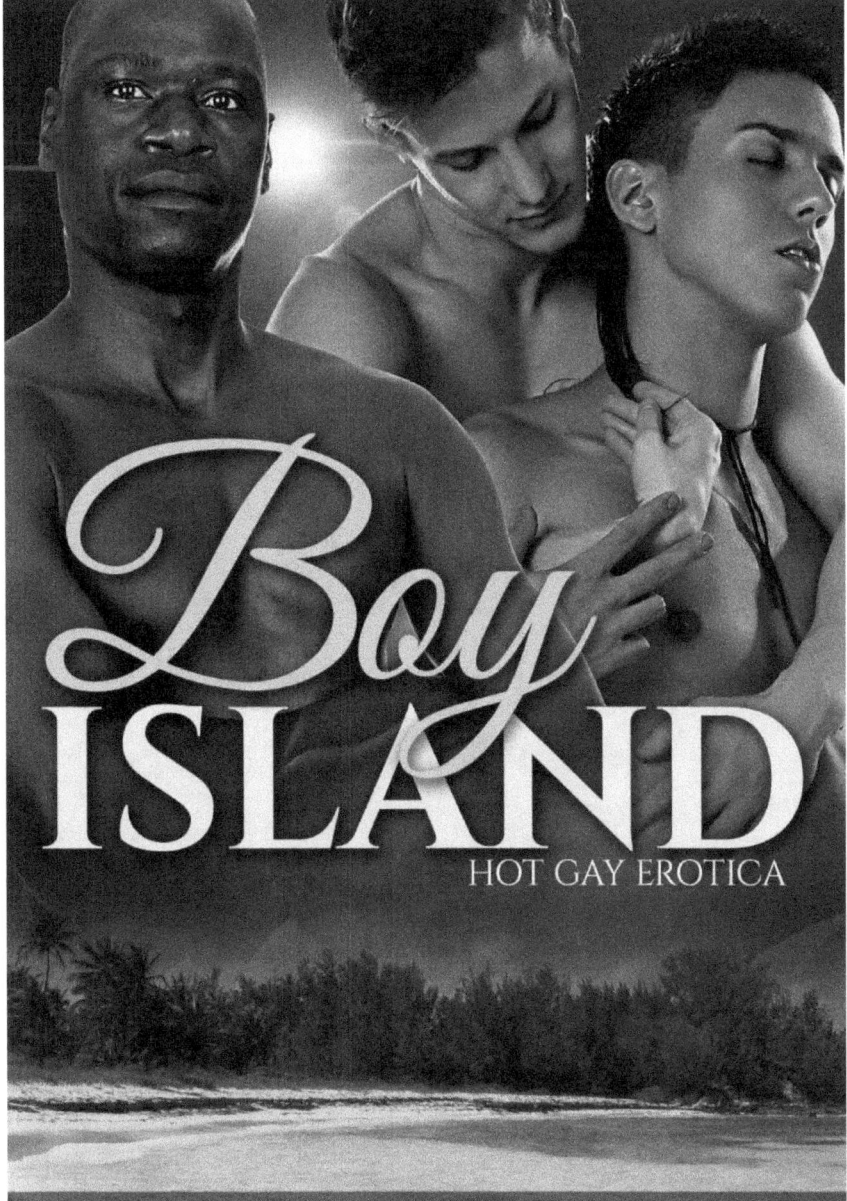

Boy ISLAND

HOT GAY EROTICA

CHRIS JOHNS

"Good, my name is Junior, I'm the boss boy here so you call me Master at all times, understand?" Topha nodded.

"My cohorts are all trained warriors to protect wimps like you from the other lot, you call them Sir, understand?" Topha was no wimp and was going to make that clear straightaway.

"I'm no wimp. They can kiss my ass before I call them Sir."

"Ok, no problem." Junior nodded.

Four boys were on Topha before he had time to react stripping him of his shorts. They pinned him face down and Junior nodded at the black warrior. He discarded his loincloth and fisted himself to an erection. Topha watched and then, as he moved round behind him he realized what was going to happen. He struggled like hell until someone grabbed his balls and squeezed hard. Result was compliance, but the scream as his anus was pierced by the black rod could be heard all over the island. He was fucked until the black stud orgasmed inside him, and then all of the warriors kissed an ass cheek before releasing him.

"They have all kissed your ass, now you call them Sir, but first, you thank Leo for putting you in your place, you'll be our fuck slut until we decide if you are worth something better."

Topha was almost traumatized by his ass fucking but did as he was told. He had never felt pain like he had just endured until his ass adapted to the invasion. He eyed up Leo who looked older than the others.

"Yes Topha, take a good look. Leo is our champion, the oldest inhabitant of the island. He can fuck more ass in one session than anyone else, piss me off again and we will get him to try to beat his previous record, but just using you."

That was good enough for Topha. He was now determined to comply with any order whatever it was. He didn't want that black monster roaming around inside him again.

Leo was a typical black with short tight curly hair, some hair on his chest and legs and in the center a cock that had to be a good ten inches long, maybe more. He had a good body and looked to be about thirty, odd as this was supposed to be 'Boy Island'. Stood again he felt too much shame to look at any of the other warriors. He was marched back to the enclosure and saw what was going to be his home for the next two years. It looked like a mediaeval village in England. He remembered from his history books what they looked like. Shown to a hut, he was introduced to another naked boy.

"Damian, look after the new boy. Clean him up and have him at my hut in two hours' time." Damian scanned Topha with his eyes before speaking.

"I'm Damian, I see you were the same as me, got stroppy with the Master. I suppose Leo fucked you." Topha looked at this boy and decided he was going to like him.

"Hello, I'm Topha, and you're right. A painful introduction to my new life."

"Well, I've got two hours to try and help you not get any more punishment. Come on, let's get you showered. The two things we have plenty of here are water and soap."

Damian was eighteen, the same as Topha, mixed race, medium build with a very prominent penis. Below the waist he was quite hairy but there was little above. Topha noticed the cock because it had started to get hard.

"Sorry Topha, I love colored guys, and you are pretty special to look at."

"Are you queer then?"

"Huh, everyone is queer on this island, or they're celibate, and there aren't many of them. Who do you think we are going to have sex with?" Topha blushed. This was not what he expected at all.

"After we shower I have to give you lessons in how to suck cock unless you are already good at it."

"No way Jose, I don't suck cock." Damian looked at this boy and wondered if he would be given to the Premier Clan.

"The Master will have you strung up and whipped before he lets Leo loose on you again unless you do as he asks. He will want you to give him a blowjob when I take you to him. If you aren't very good you will know pain like you've never known before."

Less and less Topha liked this place. He wanted to rebel again in the shower when Damian started washing his ass, particularly down the crack.

"I have to do this in case the Master wants to fuck you as well."

"I'm going to survive here Damian so I guess I have to go along with whatever they want."

Damian patted Topha's cheek. "Good boy, the better you are, the more likely they are to be gentle with you, but be prepared for a load of humiliation to start with as well as some pretty rough sex, and pray for a new boy to come quickly so that he can take your place."

If you enjoyed this sample then look for **Boy Island.**

Also by this Author:

Brotherly Love

Underworld

Revenge of the Jocks

Indian Abduction

Pleasurable Abduction

Lost

A Grip in Deep

Bullet Holes

Gay Porn Star

Delightfully Yours

Embracing the Greener Side

Promotional Desire

Aviator's Hidden Turbulence

Almost Paradise

The Hardcore Remedy

Relish Pretender

Doctor Boner

Captivated Attractions

Academically Horny

Flight of the Hornies

Empire's Desire

Erotic Physical Examination

Mauled by My Mate

Stage of Desire

Gray Pride

Billionaire Gay Lover

Picture Perfect

Greek Romance

Lights, Camera, ACTION!

My Best Bud, My Master

Hardcore Commando

I Sacrifice My Virginity for Love

Officer Hostile

The School Punisher

Undercover Pain

Antigua Romance

Guarded Emotion

Professor Voyeur

Probation Plebe

Underground Soldiers

The Body Search

Poker Slave

Cupid's Huge Arrow

Desirable Lover

A Wonderful Love

Center Stage

A Scavenger for Love

Chasing Heaven

Rent Boy

Intense Lust

Adopted Soldier

The Gym Challenge

Cry Baby

Model Wanted

A Heart on Hold

Blissful Love

Memories

Little Nympho

Losing Hope for Pleasure

The Curse of Beauty

Training the Naked Waiter

Blackmail Initiation

Search and Rescue

From the Author

If you want any more info about me, please feel free to ask! I'm a very open person so you won't offend me if you want to get more personal.

If you'd like to give me comments or suggestions to any of my books, feel free to shoot me an email at chris_johns@awesomeauthors.org.

Check my page on Amazon and my blog for Updates and interesting info.

Author Central – http://amzn.to/185Sar5
Author Blog - http://chris-johns.awesomeauthors.org/

If you enjoyed any of my books then please share the love and click like on my books in Amazon.

If you write me a review and send me an email I will send you a free book, or many.
(Just know that these emails are filtered by my publisher.)

Good news is always welcome.

One Last Thing, for Kindle Readers...

When you turn the page, Kindle will give you the opportunity to rate this book and share your thoughts on Facebook and Twitter. If you enjoyed my writings, would you please take a few seconds to let your friends know about it? Because... when they enjoy they will be grateful to you and so will I.

Thank You!

Chris Johns
chris_johns@awesomeauthors.org

About the Author

The author has drawn from his lifetime experiences as a Marine Engineer and Helicopter Pilot to take his readers round the world with his erotic stories.

Born in a small town in middle England he joined the Royal Navy straight from school and spent four years at engineering college before going to sea. After promotion to first engineer he took a career turn and trained as a helicopter pilot. The move afforded him huge opportunity to travel both as a Naval Pilot and later as a Commercial Helicopter Pilot. His Bio Pic was taken when he was relaxing in his company's social club, serving his fellow pilots and engineers with some excellent English Ale.

Retired now in the Caribbean he took up writing to compliment his other great love, sailing.

www.ingramcontent.com/pod-product-compliance
Lightning Source LLC
Chambersburg PA
CBHW060743180626
46819CB00001B/75

* 9 7 8 1 6 2 7 6 1 9 4 4 8 *